To TWA — I hope you enjoy this Book!!!
Rick

I Don't Believe You Said That

by

Rick Henderson

This book is a work of non-fiction. Names of people and places have been changed to protect their privacy.

First published by AuthorHouse 07/29/04

ISBN: 1-4184-8246-3 (e-book)
ISBN: 1-4184-3623-2 (Paperback)

This book is printed on acid free paper.

To Avy,

Without your encouragement, support and love,
this endeavor would not have taken place.
I love you the way you have been, the way you are
and the way you will be.
I will always love you.

R.H.

Table of Contents

"All In A Day's Work"

Our agency doesn't normally like to accept credit cards over the phone. I made a reservation for a client over the phone and advised him that he could fax us the credit card with a written authorization from himself allowing our agency to charge to his credit card. He said he would do it right away. Well I did not hear from him to see if he was still interested in that ticket he purchased. He said he was but when he tried to send us his credit card it wouldn't fix in his fax machine and got stuck.!! Indianapolis, IN

I just had a woman call and tell me that she had read in our Ad that we provided Amtrak Services. When I assured her that we did, she asked if that included picking her up at her home and transporting her to Amtrak station three hours away.!! Killeen, TX

Sometime ago I had a secretary call for a hotel in Los Angeles. I asked what area and, of course, she had no idea. I found a good rate at a hotel by Knots Berry Farms. When I advised her of this, there was silence. I asked her if she wanted to check with her boss as she kept referring to him. And she said, "I don't think he wants to be way out in the country".!! Chesapeake, VA

A client phoned in today and requested flights from Cincinnati to Chicago. I asked her if she would prefer Chicago O'Hare or Chicago Midway? Her reply was, "I would prefer Chicago, Illinois, please."!! Mitchell, KY

Everyone has clients with strange preferences. My favorite is a client who prefers "ODD" numbered hotel rooms—when asked why, he replied, "Because I'm left handed".!! Jacksonville, FL

A client called when Continental Airlines first had the Peanut Fares come out and ask for a "Peanut Butter" Fare. I could hardly keep from laughing and kindly explained they were Peanut Fares. We both got a kick out of this and then she suddenly stopped laughing and was silent. Afraid I had gotten a bit carried away, I apologized to her and she said it was Ok, but that she was concerned about one thing...Does this mean I won't be getting my Peanut Butter and Jelly Sandwich?!! Brunswick, GA

An agency is located on the University campus. A student came in and asked directions to the visitors' center, which is located just down the hall from the travel agency. All of a sudden, she looks at the sign on the floor and says, "Wow, you are a travel agency, then can you tell me where the International students live?"!! Madison, WI

A client in Newark, New Jersey called to find out how he could get to Kennedy in New York for a meeting. He did not want to "FLY" so would I please check into Helicopter schedules. Am I missing something, don't helicopters fly too?!! Newark, NJ

A client called to book a flight and I asked him, What time did he need to leave? He said it didn't matter. I first offered him a 7:00 A.M. flight and he said that was too early. So I offered him a noon flight, he said he could not leave then. I offered him a 6:00 P.M. flight and he said that was too late. Getting a little stressed; I asked him what was the best time for him to leave? You guessed it, he said "Anytime, I guess".!! Atlanta, GA

We had a client call about taking a honeymoon. On this trip they would be crossing the International Date Line. He wondered if his future wife was going to have to take an Extra Birth Control Pill, since she would be losing a day.!! Los Angeles, CA

A lady came in after returning from her trip asking for a refund. It seems she fell asleep during the flight and woke up in time to see the breakfast cart being stowed away by the flight attendants. Since she did not eat any food she wanted that portion of her money refunded to her. I researched a bit and found that the particular airline in question spends an average of $2.79 per passenger on breakfast. I gave her the number of the airline customer service but felt like offering her a cup of coffee and a doughnut.!! San Francisco, CA

A client wanted to change his return flight. After checking availability, there was only one seat left. We're in luck. There's only one seat left, I will grab it, "She responded is it an aisle?"!! Las Vegas, NV

We've had quite a few computer systems errors at our office lately. Mostly delayed responses. There is one client who is especially picky about his seats and, of course is a frequent flyer. A fellow agent tried to pull up the seat map for this man and an unusual response followed: It said, "Closet". I wonder if these computers have a mind of their own.!! Longwood, FL

I recently made reservations for two business women travelling from Seattle to Los Angeles. I was speaking with their travel arranger asking the usual questions regarding flight times, special meals, etc. When I asked for their seating preference, the travel arranger hesitated, then said, "Well, both of them are short, as a matter of fact, they are rather "Untall" so it doesn't matter where they sit. I wonder if I should have booked them "Unwindows" across from each other.!! Bellevue, WA

A lady who was in her 90's wanted to book a flight from Los Angeles to New York. After complaining about the schedules at great lengths, she decided on a flight and then stated she would need assistance. I said I could arrange for an electric cart for her. She then got very tickled. About the time she reached the door to leave, she turned back and said very seriously, "I don't know how to drive an electric cart. Could you teach me before I go"? She then left in her restored 1966 Mustang—clear the way!! Ashville, NC

I had a strange call a couple of weeks ago from a man who wanted to fly his kids from Minneapolis to Orlando to visit for Christmas. Not an unusual request until he said they didn't know each other. He told me these two adult children know he is their father, but neither knows they have a sibling. He told me to seat them together on the flights in the hope that they would get to talking and compare notes and find out they are brother and sister. I tried to discourage him from doing this, but he thinks it will be a great Christmas surprise for them to find out on a plane that they are related. Guess he'll have some explaining to do if they both bring a good book to read on the plane instead.!! Minneapolis, MN

Recently a client booked a reservation and said she would come in and pick up the ticket and pay by cash. Later that day she came in carrying a box. She proceeded to tell me she had been collecting these coins since they were made for one year. His ticket was for $575.00 and she paid me in Susan B Anthony dollars. Everyone in the office got a kick out of this!! Little Rock, AR

Just last week a client called and asked for a flight number for one of his co-workers. I gave it to him and then he asked, "If in this day and age with phones on the planes, could he call his co-worker on the plane now that he has his flight number. Well I really wanted to say, Well he's in seat number 11G, so the number to his seat is 555-1234.!! Farmington, MA

One Friday afternoon must have been another full moon! I received a call from an irate woman. She told me she had been trying for almost two hours to obtain a simple phone number and could not get any help. I asked her what phone number she was looking for and she replied, "THE AIRLINE". After a couple of additional questions, she told me the airline was "Eastern". I put her on hold to catch my breath and stop laughing. When I picked up, I explained that Eastern had not been operating for a number of years but I would be glad to check another airline schedule for her. Click! She hung up!! Salisbury, NC

A client's mother is paying for her daughter to take a cruise. The cruise line required a copy of the purchaser's driver's license. I spoke to the client's mother and told her to fax me a copy of the license. Two days later, the daughter brought me the actual license. She told me her mother had a hard time faxing the license since it was too small and would not fit the fax machine.!! Tiverton, RI

A new secretary from a corporate account of ours actually asked me if the Boss' morning constitution was on file with us? When I told her the AM commuter plane he was booked on had no bathroom. Embarrassing Moments!! Worthington, OH

I recently received a phone call from a gate agent. She was a bit puzzeled as my client had arrived at the gate without a ticket. I had explained to my client that this type of ticket had to be picked up at our office. The agent then put the client on the phone, who replied "No one ever told me I had to take my ticket to the airport"!! Los Angeles, CA

Yesterday I had a young gentlemen in my office for whom I booked a very simple reservation, Seattle to Los Angeles. I went over the entire itinerary twice just to be sure he understood everything. He assured me that everything looked straight-forward to him. Not even an hour later he called and told me there were no dates on his itinerary. I directed him to look under the heading date. He said, "There is nothing there except some code that says 24 Oct. I tried not to laugh out loud and responded that's 24 Oct.!! Port Orchard, WA

Our only male agent in the office was calling a cruise line for a rate. Because he knows the number by heart he didn't use the programmed speed dial. Well, apparently he got a little careless when he dialed because the phone line answered with some rather seductive music. Of course at first he thought the cruise line had a new on-hold music until the girl on the phone went on to say to call her and her sexy girlfriends: Dial 1-900-XXX-XXXX. The agent was a little embarrassed.!! Sioux Falls, SD

A few days ago I had a Senior Citizen ask me about discounts for rental cars in Las Vegas. I called the rental car agency and asked if they had Senior Citizen discounts. The agent immediately replied, "Yes, we do". Are they at least 25 years of age with a major credit card? I didn't know Senior Citizens had to be only 25.!! San Antonio, TX

I got a call from one of our attorney's secretaries. She said Mr. Attorney had lost his ticket. She went on to say the airlines gave him a lost ticket application, but he lost that too. I wanted to say to her, "I'm glad he's not my attorney".!! Las Vegas, NV

A customer called to get a quote from Seattle to St Louis. He wanted the lowest fare leaving on a Friday night. After telling him the restrictions and the fare I said he would have to stay over a Saturday night. His reply was, I would be leaving on a Friday and returning on Sunday—would this constitute a Saturday night stay?

After chuckling to myself, I said, Sir, Saturday is between Friday and Sunday.!! Los Angeles, CA

A client wanted to change his return flight. After checking availability, there was only one seat left. We're in luck. There's only one seat left, I will grab it. She responded, "Is it an aisle"?!! Las Vegas, NV

"Anything Goes"

We sponsored A Globus Gateway Night for our clients several months ago. We had a drawing at the end for a $100 Gift Certificate to be used toward future booking. Well, the lady who won the certificate called several weeks later and wanted to book at another agency. She wanted to use the certificate there. Obviously, we said she could not do that. But she never booked with us!! Bel Air, MD

Today, I had a woman call and ask what the rate was roundtrip from Bradford, PA (BFD) to Raleigh-Durham, NC (RDU) for a two week advance. I told her the roundtrip cost would be $189 on US Air. The client then said, "Didn't the fares drop because of the crash? Does she think every time a house catches fire that the mortgage rates drop too?!! Bradford, PA

I recently had an elderly client asking about fares to New Orleans (MSY). The fares were somewhat high at the time and he seemed a bit discouraged. I explained that if he was 62 or over, he and his wife could get a 10% discount. Raising his eyebrows in surprise he replied, "Oh no"! I'm not 6 foot 2. I could just imagine the gate agent standing by the jet with a tape measure!! Seaford, DE

I had a well-traveled client call for a rate to Panama City. I quoted the fare and he thought it was very high and said he would check around. He called me back the next day very angry saying the competition could get a fare for $300 less. He informed me that I was overcharging him and he would use the other travel agency from now on. Two weeks later he showed up in my office with flowers to apologize. I asked him what happened? He got the ticket from the other agency, got on the plane and thought the plane was very small but never paid any attention, flew less than an hour and landed. He asked the flight attendant what was wrong and had taken the trip many times and had never gotten there this quick. She replied, "The flight to Panama City, Florida always takes this length of time". The problem was he was going to Panama City, Panama. Moral of the story is if it sounds too good to be true, it is too good to be true.!! Spring Hill, FL

I thought I had heard it all! My client called wanting the most direct flight from Madison, Wisconsin to West Palm Beach, Florida. I explained she could either take a direct flight with two stops or a flight with one change of plane in Atlanta, which would be the most convenient? She then asked me if I could call the airline and explain to them that her 83 year old Mother was traveling alone and to make a more direct flight. Also to find out what the statistics are on flights changing their schedules. What a riot!!! Madison, WI

I had an elderly lady call me the other day wanting a roundtrip airfare from Milwaukee to Florida. I asked her where in Florida she wanted to fly and there was dead silence. Then I heard her rummaging around and muttering, "I know I have the street address around here somewhere". I covered my mouthpiece and had a laugh. Then I explained to her that I needed the city she had to fly into!! Beaver Dam, WI

I had a funny tale to tell. The day was almost over and I was making a reservation for a client. A lady called. She had just gotten her flight itinerary in the mail and had a question. The invoice was normal computer issued itinerary and it had stated on the invoice that breakfast would be served. She asked me if that meant we would be stopping to eat. True. True. She really did ask!!! Springfield, MO

An older gentlemen called our agency to help him with his travel arrangements from Los Angeles. After about an hour of trying to get his approval on anything, the agent finally succeeded. She thanked him for calling, yet he remained silent. When she asked him if there was anything else, he became a bit upset, then he said, "Well,

I was waiting for you to tell me what time you will pick me up for the airport".!! Ventura, CA

After a somewhat late Friday night, I knew it was going to be a challenge when a client called wanting to fly from Moline, Iowa to Texas. Where to Maam, I asked"? "To Texas" she replied. I knew she wasn't getting my drift so I tried to be as specific as possible. "Yes, I understand Maam, but where in Texas did you want to fly into"? She answered with a very put out, "Why the airport, of course"!! Rock Island, IL

I had an elderly woman come in for an airline ticket from Chicago, O'Hare Airport to Tampa, Florida. She had called an airline reservation number and gotten prices. She now wanted to purchase a ticket. I asked her the date she wanted to leave which she gave me and I told here what time the flights were. She replied, "No, I want to leave at 2 PM". When I explained there were no flights leaving at that time, she confidently assured me that the airline said she could fly anytime on Saturday for that price and she wanted to leave at 2 PM!! Charles, IL

A client called and had a Delta small fare coupon for $79.00 each way. I advised here the fare would be $158.00 roundtrip, but she would have to pay a $2.50 refueling charge and a $6.00 passenger facility charge. She replied, "Oh my, they charge you just for using the bathroom. How rude". I told her that was a good one!! Stoneham, MA

I swear this is a true story: A client came in asking about "Coach" fares. I thought this strange since most want the lowest prices possible. He wanted to go Dulles to Seattle so, of course, the price was over $1,000.00. He exclaimed that's not much of a discount. I told him there were cheaper rates, but he did ask for coach fares. To this he replied, "Well, I am a high school basketball coach and I'm shocked that the airlines would want to squeeze that kind of money out of us"!! I tried so hard not to laugh and explained to him that a "Coach" fare is not

an employee discount. What will they think of next"?!!
Houston, TX

I just had a call from a secretary checking on her boss's flight from Huntsville, Alabama to Orlando, Florida with a connection in Atlanta. She wanted to know how long was his "Hangover" in Atlanta.!! Shrewbury, NJ

A woman called for the rate to Orlando. After quoting her the lowest rate, she said she would think about it and call back. About an hour later she called back and she wanted me to make her a reservation. She said she had checked with the airline direct and was quoted $6.00 more than I had given her. When she questionned the reservation agent, she was told that the $6.00 was a facility charge by the connecting airport. She then told me, "I can't believe the airport would charge me to use the facilities. I always use the airplane facilities and have never been charged"!! After catching my breath and composing myself, I explained the charge was actually a passenger facility charge that certain airports impose to help with airport improvements.!! South Bend, IN

Sometimes you think you have heard it all until yesterday! Our office manager was going over some prices for a client wanting an all-inclusive package from Montreal (YMX) to Acapulco (ACA). When the client asked if they could just get a "Drink Plan" since they would be drinking all day and wouldn't feel like eating"!! Plattsburg, NY

I recently took a weekend trip with my boyfriend. This was his first time on a plane. In Dallas-Fort Worth, we had to have the plane de-iced for our flight back to St Louis. He turns and asks me while they are de-icing the plane, "Why are they washing the plane now? Everyone on the plane within hearing distance lost it!! Fenton, MO

A company we work with brings people into town and we do the reservations. One of these clients is a real pain and you wonder how he walks around without help! His latest escapade happened this morning. He called to say he needed help. It seems he turned too soon into the hotel and ended up on the median and he was afraid to try to get off. Could we please come get him off? We called the rental company to assist him. When he came into our office, he informed us not to rent him a Taurus any more. It seems they are too low to the ground!!! Birmingham, AL

After a rather hectic day, a lady dashed into our office just before closing and asked, "Do you have one of those machines that tells when a flight is due into a City"? Before I could stop myself I said, "Yes, Maam, it's called a computer!! Atlanta, GA

A few years ago, I worked for a large agency on the 24 hour Traveler Assistance Hotline. Needless to say, we had the cream of the crop call in. One Saturday evening I was working and received a call from a lady traveling on business in Los Angeles. I was based out of Ohio.

A thousand miles away. She was calling me from her hotel room and told me there was somebody looking in her window. I asked if she had called Security and she replied, "No, you made the reservation for me so I thought I should call you". After I called the hotel front desk for her and had them send Security to her room, I asked her what room she was in and she said 424. I called the front desk agent back to tell him and we both laughed so hard. She was on the fourth floor.!! Dayton, OH

I made an air reservation a while back for a lady flying to Miami. When I told here that lunch would be served, she asked me if I knew which restaurant they would be stopping at along the way! She honestly thought that the plane would land and everyone would get off to go to a restaurant for lunch and then get back on the plane and continue to Miami.!! Madison, WI

We received a call from a client that spends a great deal of time thinking of exotic places he would love to travel to if he had lots of money. He always ends up with

an inexpensive air/land package that is on special. One day I suggested a special to the Bahamas that had come across the fax. He wanted to make sure that he could stay on the Beach. I advised him the hotel I was booking was on the Beach. He then said that he didn't think I understood that he wanted to stay on the Beach. I tried to explain again that, although this was a hotel that could fit into his price range, it was on the Beach, although not deluxe or exotic. He then said, "No, I don't want a hotel. I want to sleep on the Beach". I explained they didn't allow that and it was not considered exotic but idiotic.!!
Bridgeport, PA

I received a frantic call from a passenger that had missed his scheduled flight. He was very upset because his meeting went longer than he had anticipated. He asked me what time was the next flight from Los Angeles to St Louis and if he could fly standby with no penalties. After checking, I confirmed there were seats available. I told the passenger to get to the airport as soon as possible since standbys were on a first come, first serve basis. After a very long pause, the passenger then asked if I get on this flight does this mean that I have to stand all the way from Los Angeles to St Louis"? After my hysterical laughter subsided, I assured him that he would have a seat if he made the flight.!! (Rick Henderson) Los Angeles, CA

I was booking a reservation for my husband's Grandmother who has traveled only three times in her life. The doctor advised here that she should have oxygen on the plane in case she suffered from shortness of breath. Well, she did not want to have to buy oxygen and wanted to know if she could just reach up and pull down the oxygen mask that the airlines provides. It took some explaining to convince her that this was for emergency use only and could not be accessed any other way.!! Dayton, OH

"Bags and Baggage"

When I first became a travel agent, I booked a reservation for a woman traveling internationally. This was not only her first trip internationally, but it was her first time flying as well. I issued her tickets and she went on her way. About a month went by and the lady called me back. She said that she was terribly embarrassed and began to tell me her story. Apparently, she had read the information regarding how many checked bags she could have and when she arrived at the airport to check in for her flight, she gave the agent at the counter a very hard time. She exploded on him about how many stores and how long it took her to find "checked bags". It was not what she had taken it to be!! Houston, TX

One of my clients told me the following story: He was flying from Austin (AUS) to San Francisco (SFO) and he checked his retriever to fly in his kennel as cargo. His flight required a connection in Dallas and after he boarded his connection he saw a dog similar to his running across the runway into the grassy area. At first he was horrified to think it was his dog, but decided it couldn't be his dog. He didn't think about it again until he claimed his dog in San Francisco and his dog was covered with burrs and grass. Apparently his dog got out of the cage while being transferred. One wonders how he got back in safely!! Austin, TX

How about the client when told she is allowed two pieces of checked baggage come up with "I only have gray and furthermore, I do not like stripes or checks"!! Lansing, MI

A client called me from Tucson. He couldn't remember where he parked his car at the airport when he flew out. He asked, "Do you know where it is"?!! Phoenix, AZ

Today a lady wanted me to tell her which week in February she would be able to see the most whales off Maui!! Lancaster, WI

A friend of mine works for an airline. Recently helping out an international customer she asked, "What kind of passport are you holding"? The passenger's response: "A Blue One"!! Miami, FL

I called a resort in Vermont to ask the price for a golf and lodging package. The reservationist asked me, "Do they plan to play on the golf course"? I can't imagine where else they would play golf!! East Hartford, CT

I had a client call and buy four (4) tickets. Each ticket was for a different person and had a different price. I called the client back to give him the total for the four tickets. I asked him whether he would like the prices separated or just one grand total. He replied, "Which is cheaper"?!! Pratt, KS

Here's my craziest client story: I booked a husband and wife on a roundtrip to Miami. On all four legs I was able to get them a two-across aisle/window. When they got back, I called them to find out how their trip went. I was horrified, then hysterical when the husband informed me that I was the worst travel agent he had ever dealt with. He had specifically told me that he liked aisle seats and his wife preferred the window and that I booked them backwards on two of the flights. I guess he never figured out that they could change seats with each other!! Huntsville, AL

I had an elderly client going from Pittsburgh to Phoenix and I went over her itinerary completely in the office. About an hour after she left she called. She couldn't understand what her flight number was. His seat was 9F and her flight was number 9. She then asked if she changed her seat to 10F, would the flight number be 10. I tried not to laugh as I explained that one had nothing to do with the other!! Sewickly, PA

Years ago when I was working with Allegheny Airlines, I had to board a passenger with a seeing-eye dog. I told the agent in the terminal to keep the passengers inside the terminal until I boarded the passenger. As I was about to go into the plane, I asked the captain who was at the foot of the stairs to hold onto the dog until I seated the passenger and then I would come out to get the dog. Well, the agent in the terminal let the passengers out to the plane a little too soon while I was still in the plane. Well, the sight they saw was frightening. The Captain was standing next to the stairway holding a seeing-eye dog wearing dark sunglasses. I had a hard time convincing the passengers to board that plane!! Jamestown, NY

When you think you've heard it all, you pick up the phone and a client asks if you do tours to the Netherlands with assisted suicide as part of the package. This client was totally serious. When I informed him that we don't handle that type of package, he wanted to know what a one-way and one roundtrip would cost to Amsterdam. I replied, "When will you be departing"? He answered, "In two weeks". He also wanted to verify that he could receive assistance at the gate. I asked him what type of assistance he needed and he stated—"A Stretcher!! Where is Dr Kevorkian when you need him!! Arbor, MT

A lady came into book her "dead" husband's body and herself from Little Rock, Arkansas to Raleigh-Durham via Atlanta. After her return, she came in screaming because the body was delayed in Atlanta for three hours and he almost missed his own funeral. She later came in and apologized knowing it was not the agent's fault and brought her cookies as an "I'm sorry" gift.!! Conway, AR

A woman in our office was trying to book a hotel in Atlanta for a client but was not having any success because of the complex convention. When she explained the reason for being unable to book a room, the client was shocked and said, "They definitely would not be coming to Atlanta because they refused to go anywhere that had a "convict" convention!! Marietta, GA

"Cruising"

One day a couple came in with questions regarding their cruise. They were all good questions except for when the husband asked, "Now when we get off the plane in Miami, in what terminal and gate will the ship be and how long of a walk is it"? Thinking they were pulling my leg, I laughed, then realized I was laughing alone. They were dead serious.!! Bridgeton, NJ

I had some first time cruisers call me and say that a friend told them that they would have to reserve and pay for the use of the deck chairs for their cruise. I really had to hold back the laughter!! Milwaukee, WI

I recently had a customer requesting prices on the cruise including Walt Disney World and the Bahamas! After giving the information and talking about the required travel arrangements she asked, "Isn't there one that leaves right from Disney World? I don't want to go

all the way over there"!! I don't think she believed us.!!
Hampton, NH

An elderly woman called to make arrangements
to attend her grandson's wedding in Honolulu. After
checking numerous options, we finally agreed on an
itinerary. When I informed her of the price, she asked, "Is
that in U.S. or Hawaiian dollars"?!! Minneapolis, MN

On my first cruise, I overheard a passenger who had
a cabin in the rear of the ship ask the Cruise Director,
"Does the elevator near my cabin take me up to the front
of the ship"?!! Marion, OH

I had a client this morning who began by telling me
that she gets seasick and she is going on a cruise next
month. She went to her Doctor to get a prescription for
a patch and he had no idea what they were or where to
obtain them. After a long time of not having a clue on what
information she was trying to get from me, she finally
asked me if we sold that at our office! It's amazing what

people think a travel agent's job description includes. Like a medical degree to prescribe drugs!! Newark, NJ

A favorite question of mine is from clients to ask, "What time does this cruise take off from Orlando"? when they book a Disney Cruise Package. I kindly say, first you have to drive to the ocean!! Monroe, MI

After booking a cruise for a married couple, I started explaining to the wife about prices. I told her that she was in a category four (4) and she said to me, "I only want to be in a cabin with my husband and not four other people"!! Greensboro, NC

We have a client that enjoys traveling quite often. Last year he went to the <u>Grand Canyon</u> and when he got home he told a friend about the great time he had. He'd been there the year before on a <u>cruise.</u> When he told me this story, I questionned it and he told me that she had actually been to <u>Grand Cayman</u>!! Mineola, NY

A woman called our office and wanted to know about a cruise to Las Vegas. Assuming she meant a charter air package, I began to give her options. I knew we weren't on the same wave-length when she began asking about cabin stewards. I told her she couldn't cruise to Las Vegas because it was land-locked in the middle of the desert. She replied, "It is"? Oh well, how about a cruise to Phoenix then"?!! Prairie du Chien, WI

A few years ago when I was a Leisure Travel Agent, a gentleman called to ask about cruises. I was very excited because I was a brand new agent at this location. Of course I started telling him about all of the Carribean cruise specials that we had and so on. He then asked me a question that blew me away. He told me he was only interested in cruises that were to Las Vegas, Nevada!! It took me a v-e-r-y l-o-n-g time to convince my client that there was "no ocean" to cruise on in Nevada!! Little Rock, AR

We have always sent a Bon Voyage gift to customers taking at least a seven-day cruise—usually a bottle of wine or champagne. It has always amazed me that very few people ever bother to say "Thank You". They just seem to take it for granted. Now I've heard everything. Some repeat customers were booking another cruise and actually had the nerve to ask that instead of the usual bottle of wine, could we please send a bottle of Scotch and a bottle of Gin!! Clemsen, SC

A man came in the other day asking about vacation spots for Honeymooners. He explained he was going to pick and purchase where his son would Honeymoon. I gave him a few suggestions, like maybe a cruise. He then cringed and said, "7 nights on a boat is too long and my son doesn't even like to fish"!! Chicago, IL

Last time I cruised on a well-known line, I overheard two elderly women get very excited when we were about to cast off. They were playing a recording of Kathie Lee Gifford singing the well known theme song. One woman turned to me and said, "Isn't it nice that she's here for the cruise. I wonder what night she's going to entertain"? Time for a reality check!! North Reading, MA

A client called me last week and wanted to take a Greek Island Cruise. I advised her there are 7-day cruises and that she could spend two nights in Athens, either before or after the cruise. She asked me why would she stay in Athens . . . doesn't the cruise leave from Miami"?!! Summit, NJ

I just had a call from a woman who wanted to know, "How much does it cost to take a four (4) day cruise from Los Angeles through the Panama Canal"?!! Laguna Hills, CA

"Did You Really Say That"?

We have a charter bus company along with our travel agency. Recently a lady called to charter one of our buses to Lancaster, Pennsylvania. She wanted a lot of information but the one request that we all lost it on was when she asked, "Is it possible to go when all the Amish people aren't out"?!! Everett, PA

I know travel agents are supposed to know general sightseeing information about an area, but was surprised by a woman yesterday who wanted a list of flea markets in the neighborhood. She was a little indignant that I could not provide this!! Pittsburgh, PA

This morning a client called requesting rates for hotels in St Croix and Aruba. She wanted something scheduled but not so secluded that her "18-month old baby would have nothing to do"!! Staten Island, NY

king in Las Vegas around the time

ne to town, I had a call from a guy

servations. I replied, yes, and then

e him a campsite at Lake Mead.

ow that is a Dead Head I thought!! Carson City, NV

I always read about those stories about clients but how about those fellow travel industry employees. I just hung up with a major airline. I needed to check free seats to St Thomas. He answered, "Oh, in the Bahamas". And, of course, I figured he misunderstood me so I said, "No, St Thomas". He rudely replied, "Miss, St Thomas is in the Bahamas". Needless to say, I thanked him, hung up and called back to get someone else. I wonder who told him that!! Longwood, FL

I was making a car reservation for a corporate client and I asked him what size car he wanted. He replied, "A large car". I proceeded to make a reservation and told him the car would be a Lincoln Towncar or something similar. He then asked me, "What make of car is called a similar"?!! New York, NY

We had a client come into the office looking for a honeymoon to Hawaii. He narrowed down the hotel choices to three different properties and wanted us to find out if any or all of the hotels had cable stations that would broadcast the Phoenix Suns basketball games. This was how he would make his final choice. I hope he had an understanding bride!! Mesa, AZ

Every day is an adventure in this industry and any traveler, regardless of how savvy can amaze me with questions and comments that display no knowledge of travel experience. I had a client who called to inquire about an unused ticket. He said, "I purchased a non-refundable ticket a while back and I'm not going to use it. Can I get a refund"? I politely explained to him that refunds are not possible with non-refundable tickets, unless the ticketed passenger dies. He then asked if I would be willing to inform the airlines of his recent death!! The things they ask!! LaCrosse, WI

Recently a friend just completed travel to Las Vegas with her 80 year old Mother. After playing the slot machines for some time, the little old lady had won a few quarters. Realizing it was time to go to dinner, she left her daughter to go upstairs to change for dinner. She went into the elevator with her bucket of quarters and waited for the doors to close when two men got into the elevator. One man was built fairly stocky and the other man was normal size. The lady shrunk as far as she could into the corner of the elevator with her coins since she was afraid they would rob her. One of the men said, "Hit the door" to the other man. She, the lady being frightened of them in the first place thought he said, "Hit the Floor". She then threw her coins up in the air and dropped to the floor face first. When the two men realized what she had done they helped her up and collected her coins. Then they escorted her to her room. They apologized to her for scaring her and left her in her room to calm down.

The very next day, three (3) dozen roses were delivered to her room with $100 bills attached to each rose. The card read, "Thanks for the best laugh I ever had. . ., Eddie Murphy"!! Grandville, MI

I had a client call me on the car phone in his rental car to ask me how to get to the airport. I grabbed the atlas I keep handy in my desk at all times and asked him his location. He was driving at the time, so I had to work fast giving him directions on the major highway. Thankfully, he got to the airport and made his flight or I sure would have heard about it later!! Oak Brook, IL

As the in-house agent for a Government contracting company, I was a bit nervous when I learned the President of the company would be coming to my office that day to discuss hotel reservations for Baltimore-Washington. As he neared my desk I felt my blood pressure rise and my palms started to sweat. He sat down, folded his arms and gave me a blank stare. I smiled and said, "Hello, I understand you need hotel reservations for Baltimore".

He nodded. Then I asked, "Would you prefer to have one king in your bed or two queens"? He replied, "Two queens, of course"!! The ice was broken!! Norfolk, VA

In Canada they get all kinds too! The office is in a medium size mall with an open door atmosphere. We have a brochure rack head level all the way around the office with two lower racks behind the first two agents, plus a planter display rack with four rows on it. Lots of brochures in our office! A lady walks in and asks if we have any travel brochures. As we look conspiciously around, we said, "Yes, anything specific"? We then gave her a few brochures. She then wanted to know where to go to actually book the trip! Who knows!! London, Ontario, Canada

"Dollars and Sense"

I had a client call today to tell me that he wanted his friend to have the seat next to him on his flights. I asked if this agency did his reservations and he told me, "No". I then asked him what exactly was he asking me to do. He wanted me to pull up the person's name that was assigned to the seat next to him and call that person to ask if they would switch seats so he and his friend could sit together!! Newark, NJ

I've been a travel agent for 17 years and thought I'd heard everything! Foolish me! I recently had a client who had a final payment due. She called me the day after it was due to see if I had found her check "under the flower pot outside the office door" where she put it three days earlier. You know that's the first thing I do when I come in the morning is look under the flower pot!! How about you?!! Wyoming, MI

I was speaking to a client making an official business reservation. I advised the client that I would build him a profile so that I would have all of his preferences, such as seat, hotel and meals. He said, "Oh, that's great"! So does that mean the next time I need to travel you will call me"?!! Arlington, VA

About two weeks ago I booked a client on Delta to Orlando. After storing the fare I received a response from Delta telling me, do not confirm any more "Bunny Run" on this flight. Not having a clue what a "Bunny Run" was, I, of course, called Delta to find out. The agent I spoke to was not sure so he put me on hold to find out. After speaking to several managers, he got back on the line and said there was a "Rabbit Convention" in Orlando and they were at their limit on the amount of "bunnies" on the aircraft. We all had a good laugh out of that one!! Fenton, MO

I just had a client inquiring about Las Vegas. I asked her if she wanted a deluxe, moderate or middle of the road hotel. I almost lost it when she replied, "Well, as long as it's close to the shows, the middle of the road will be fine".!! St Petersburg, FL

In attempting to upgrade my client using a first class upgrade certificate, I was told by the airline reservation agent that I could only upgrade one class of service. The next class being "B", "H" or "K". Oh, what we're up against!! Staten Island, NY

I had a new corporate secretary call stating her boss just called from the airplane and he needed a rental car in Baltimore-Washington by the time his plane landed. I told her I could get him a Dollar Rent-A-Car for approximately $25.00 a day with unlimited mileage. She was quiet for a moment and said very seriously, "Why did you say it was a dollar if it cost $25.00 a day"? I started to laugh and explained that Dollar was the name of the car rental company and not the cost!! San Diego, CA

During the Southwest 25th Anniversary sale, I had a client come in wanting to book seven (7) passengers, ELP (El Paso)-LAX (Los Angeles) roundtrip. Due to the fact that we can only sell four (4) seats per record, I advised my client I could only sell four seats at a time. Before I could finish my statement, he jumped in and said, "Should I walk out and come in again so you can book the other three (3) persons!! El Paso, TX

We have our office in a town of 2,000 people that draw over 2 million visitors a year. They drive by and see the word travel and think we are the local chamber office. One afternoon a station wagon with California license plates pulls up and out comes a lady with three (3) kids ages 8-11. She sits them down at my desk and winks at me. She asks how much it would cost to send three (3) "very bad" children back to Los Angeles today one-way. The kids were making promises of being better!! Even cleaning the car and to never sing "99 bottles of beer" ever again. I punched a few keys and said, "Very cheap only $29.00 per child"!! She thanked me and said that was well worth it. Winked again and out the door they went!! I have recommended this strategy to many traveling across the country. It must work because I never did see them again!! Eureka Springs, MA

I had a lady call with one of the funniest requests for a fare I have ever heard! She wanted rates Charlotte to La Guardia and when I gave her the rates, she asked if there was something cheaper. I replied no that this was it. Then she said, "Well what about those *free bump fares* I've heard about. *I'd be willing to go to the airport and let them bump into me if I could fly somewhere free*!! Kannapolis, NC

A woman called for a hotel in Myrtle Beach, SC. When I gave her the hotel rate she replied, "I'm not going to get there until midnight, can't I pay for half a night?!! Pauling, NY

I had a client call and want to book a Mexico vacation. After doing some research, I came up with a fun trip at a good price. The client said to book it and gave me her credit card. After trying to process the card four times, I called and said they would not accept the card for that amount. She replied, "I don't understand why it doesn't work, I've been using it all week to buy new clothes". Later that day her husband came in and paid by check and said he needed to teach his wife about finances. We both had a laugh over it!! Gunnison, CO

I had a client call and ask me for a price on a round-trip ticket from Detroit to St. Louis. Well this was at the time of the $25.00 fares. So I told her it would be $56.00. She started getting all mad at me and started yelling that once she had a fare to St. Louis for $19.00 round-trip. She then proceeded to say she can't believe prices have gone up that much since 1982!! Livonia, MI

About a month ago I started to have all of the symptoms of a heart attack while at work. There is a Doctor's clinic right next door, so I called over and they said to come over immediately. The last thing the

nurse said as she was getting off the phone was, "Could you bring over my airline tickets that I purchased last week for me." No thanks to my clients, I am fine!!
Poulsbo, WA

"Embarrassing Moments!!!"

I had only been an agent for a few weeks and was the main person to answer the phone and direct calls that I could not help with. One day a call came from a lady telling me she had 20 people for Saigon. I got quite excited but not having the knowledge yet of groups going to Saigon, I turned this call over to my boss who is also the owner of the agency. He was only on the phone a few seconds when he hung up and told me she thought she called the playhouse for theater tickets to see "Miss Saigon", not Royal Poinciana travel for airline tickets to Saigon!! Palm Beach, FL

A co-worker of mine got a phone call from a client. The client's name was "Muffin". They were both talking and my co-worker received another call. She put Muffin on hold and when she came back to her she said, "OK Biscuit, thank you for holding"!! Coral Gables, FL

All of us experience temporary memory lapses and forget the name of someone we really should know. Well that very thing happened to an agent in my office recently when the time came to build the PNR (Personal Name and Record), the agent simply asked "And how do you spell your last name"? The reply was S-M-I-T-H. Unfazed, the agent said, "I thought it had an E at the end". We had a good chuckle over this!! Marysville, MO

I had a client traveling from Philadelphia to Billings, Montana. I informed her she had a change in Chicago and she asked, "What kind of clothes should I take to change into"?!! Belleville, IL

I got a call from a corporate client that thought she might have to travel overseas. She wanted to get visas for every country she could. I explained that it was impossible unless you have more information, like departure dates and cities. Most countries have a time limit from time of entry and departure. I still don't think she understood!! Minneapolis, MN

Today I received a phone call from a lady inquiring about documentation needed to enter Mexico. I proceeded to tell her the different options she had. She replied that she did have a birth certificate and picture ID, but was I sure that was all she needed. I told her that would do. She then told me a friend of hers told her she needed a credit card to enter Mexico. I was a little puzzled until she said, "You know like a Visa". Well at least we all got one good laugh before the day ended!! Sugarland, TX

"Food for Thought"

I just had an elderly lady call for the fare Pittsburgh to Tampa. I quoted her the rate and told her which airline she could take. She didn't want to fly so I suggested AMTRAK. She didn't want that either. I asked her how she wanted to travel and she said, "Can't you drive me there"?!! Lower Burrell, PA

I just quoted a woman a round trip fare of $129.00 Boston to Nashville. She was excited and thought it sounded great! Then she told me she was taking her two children along. She was truly bummed out when I had to explain that the $129.00 was per ticket and that all three of them could not travel on just one ticket!! Augusta, ME

I had a customer call today regarding two (2) adults and a 14 year old and 9 year old traveling to Rome. I told her the 14 year old would pay adult fare and the

9 year old would get a children's discount. She then asked me did they actually go by age or does size make a difference? Her 9 year old is 5 feet 4 inches tall and is actually taller than her 14 year old. This is perhaps the dumbest question I have had in 20 years, but I thought it was cute anyway!! Clemson, SC

I know you're used to reading funny things clients say, but here's a twist. This is a question asked by an agent. The agent which I will call "her" to protect her identity asked me about what qualifications you need to fly on a Business Class fare? I didn't understand the question, so I asked her to elaborate. She then replied, "I am making a reservation for two children. . . How can the airline verify they are traveling on business? I looked at her with a big question mark on my face and said, "What do you mean"? The agent replied, "If I put them in Business Class, don't they have to be traveling on business"?!! Cincinnati, OH

A very good friend of mine was traveling with her boyfriend on a night flight to San Jose, California. My friend was very tired and dozed most of the way. Every once in a while her boyfriend would say, "Man, the moon is bright". She would just nod and fall back to sleep. Finally after she woke up he said, "The moon is so bright and look it's following us". She turned to look at the moon to realize the "Moon" was actually the light on the wing of the plane. I about died when she told me that!! Omaha, NE

I am a corporate agent and at one point our receptionist needed help with a leisure call. She said it would be quick and easy so I said I would help. A man had called earlier for Eugene, Oregon to Great Falls. I thought he said Great Balls! I immediately typed it in and when nothing came up, I was kind of at a loss since the receptionist saw what I had typed and said, "No, Great Falls". It was the funny of the day!! I thought it was the Leisure Travel Hot Spot to go to!! Eugene, OR

"Geographically Speaking"

A passenger traveling from Canada to the United States said she had her birth certificate, but she hasn't had it "updated to her married name for travel"!! Grand Falls, Windsor, Newfoundland

While working at a major airline, I received a call from a frantic woman wanting to know the price a of one-way ticket from Los Angeles to Athens, Greece. After quoting the fare, she asked about the box. While attempting to go over the baggage requirements she interrupted me and again asked about the box. I told her she could bring either a suitcase or box with the proper dimensions and she again interrupted me and said, "the box", "the box"!! The one to put the lady in. *"She's dead"*. I told her to call the funeral home for the proper procedures!! Newport Beach, CA

At our agency we have a different department in which we make reservations. On this one occasion, I received a phone call in my department—Customer Service—for a woman wanting to make reservations. When I asked her if it was domestic or international she replied, "International, I'm going to North Carolina"!!
Nashville, TN

Once again there is no accounting for geographical misknowledge! This week I have been asked for schedules to Zuma with a "Z" Arizona and Orlando, California!!
Madison, WI

I live in Alaska and it amazes me how people conceive us. For example, I was sending a prepaid ticket and when the agent asked me where I was located, I stated Anchorage, Alaska. She then said, "Isn't that just outside of Salt Lake City"? When I responded, "No". She said, "Oh, that's right, you guys just became part of Canada, so I need to do this as an international prepaid"! I just could not believe it and she was so surprised when I told her that we were part of the United States and said, "You can't be!...You don't touch the rest of us"! I still laugh about that one!! Anchorage, AK

Today I had the client of all time! She came into the office and said she wanted to go to the Vatican to see a papal mass. I proceeded to call tour operators to see who offered such a program. I found all the info and she wanted to know the flight information. When I told her the arrival time in Rome, she was shocked and asked me why I was sending her to Rome when the Vatican is in Italy!! Astoria, NY

I was a relatively new agent at the time of this event and I hope I never go through anything like this again! My friend's husband was in Saudi Arabia during Desert Storm. A friend of her husband was also and had a serious heart attack. She called me at home to see if I could get her a ticket to Frankfort, Germany that leaves early in the morning. I went down to the office and booked the ticket. I asked her if she had a passport and she stated she didn't. She had special Government orders that waived the need for one. The next morning I told my manager what had happened and she said it didn't matter, she still needed to have a passport. Well, she had already left, so I tried to have her paged, then dialing directly to the counter to catch her before she boarded. In the meantime, I tried to get a passport faxed to her, but the office was closed due to Arbor Day. I started making calls at 8:30AM and talked to every Government agency coast to coast. Knowing her flight had just departed, I called the counter to talk to my client. To my surprise there was a mixup and she was allowed to board without a passport. I left the office at 7:30PM. The National Guard sent me an official certificate of appreciation for my distinguished contributions to the National Defense. Isn't that a hoot!! Fremont, NE

I work for an airline consolidator and I got a call from an agent who was desperately trying to find a package deal to Guadalajara, Mexico that included airfare and a nice room with an ocean view. I think she will be searching for a long time!! Portland, OR

I called one of our local tour companies wanting to check on car rental prices for McAllen in Corpus Christie, Texas. I first asked for the price for McAllen. The agent paused and said, "That's in Florida"? I said, "No, it's in Texas and he said, "Oh" and laughed. Then I asked about Corpus Christie. He said, "Now that's in Florida"! I said, "No, that's in Texas, too"! He replied laughing and saying, "You know I never really was good in Geometry"! I almost died laughting!! Elk River, MN

A few days ago an agent in our office received a phone call from a lady who wanted to go to California. The agent said, "Great, what part of California"? After a brief pause, the client said, "Oh, I don't know. Close to Seattle or Cincinnati, I guess"! The agent handled this very well simply by saying Ohio. The client's response was only, "OK, that's fine wherever". After the conversation we had a good laugh but did hope that she wasn't

traveling alone. Who knows where she would end up!!
Gloucester, VA

I had a client call the other day who wanted to go
to St Thomas in the Virginia Islands. It gave me a
laugh I needed during one of those typical Mondays!!
Houston, TX

A woman called in and wanted to fly from Los Angeles
to Chicago. When I asked her whether she wanted
to fly into O'Hare or Midway, she responded with,
"Which one is closest to Detroit"? She did indeed end
up booking a reservation to Detroit and not Chicago!!
St Charles, MO

"Please Be Seated"

We were finishing up a really busy Thursday afternoon when I received a call from a client we often fly cross-country. It seems he was complaining about his seat being too far back in the plane and he was ranting and raving about the fact. I explained the rules about seat assignments and what the airplanes allow travel agents to assign with respect to Frequent Flyer priorities i.e., Emergency Exits. And, I further explained that we did the best we could. I suggested that he try at the airport to have someone reassign his seat. He just went on and on about how awful the seat was. Jammed up against the end of the plane and the noise was terrible and the plane was full, so the steward could do nothing and he finally complained that the static on the phone was so bad it was preventing him from hearing me. I took a quick look at his record and realized he was calling from the plane and expected me to change his seat!! Old Tappan, NJ

I was making a reservation for a man to fly to Lima, Peru. He travels all over the world and is a tour guide for a group called "Wings" which are a bunch of watchers that look for anything rare in the sky, such as Birds, etc. Well, he started asking me for specific seats. He started talking faster than the men at the auctions. He said, "No Middles" aisles up front on right side . . . or windows outside. . . Okay did you get that"? I said sure, I confirmed that window on the "outside" for you. Do you mind if it makes you have a bad hair day? He laughed and said, "My dear, sometimes you just have to spread your "Wings" and "Fly"!! Tucson, AZ

I received a call from a young woman I booked on a seven day trip to London. She wanted to be sure she could use her American Express card in London because she was not sure if she could apply for the London Express card in time for her trip!! Boston, MA

Many years ago I started my career as a city ticket office agent. An elderly lady came into pick up her ticket and I was told that she had never flown before. As she turned to leave she said, "Please make sure I have a seat on the plane because I am not able to stand for that long a time"!! Montgomery, AL

I had a woman call to get information on some flights. I gave her prices and she asked me to book the flight. I advised her it was sold out. No seats available. She responded, "That's OK, I'll stand"!! Wheeling, IL

While working the after hours service one evening, I received a call from a gentleman who wanted to know if the airplane was going to land at their designated destination or if due to weather they would be rerouted. The gentleman was calling me from the *"airplane"*. . .and that is what I asked him after he posed his question. . . "You're on the plane"?!! Salt Lake City, UT

I recently asked a client if he would perfer a window or an aisle seat. He then asked me which would cost less. I told him that they were the same price. He then told me that he wanted whichever was cheaper!! Just goes to show you that people do not listen to you!! Los Alamos, NM

I was recently on a flight to Las Vegas and was witness to a rather odd situation. A couple came to the seats across the aisle from me where their assigned seats were and found a woman already seated in one of the seats. They explained that they had that seat but the woman refused to move claiming it was her seat and they would have to go somewhere else. They all took out their boarding passes and sure enough she had the same seat number. I leaned over and asked to see the boarding passes and found that the woman seated had a pass for the flight that had left two hours earlier that day!!! Same airline...same seat!! When the flight attendant came over she asked the woman to get off the plane so her situation could be resolved. She put up a fight but finally left. As she started down the aisle, she turned to the couple and said, "Don't get too comfortable, I'll be back"! What some people will do for that perfect seat!! Wayne, IL

Today I had a client request a "Bucket' seat on the plane. Of course she meant "bulkhead".!! Atlantic City, NJ

I had a gentleman asking about one way fares from Halifax, Nova Scotia, Canada to Calgary, Alberta, Canada and just before I shocked him with an expensive price. I jokingly asked him if he was sitting down. He replied, "Well I don't have to if it's cheaper to fly standing up in the plane!! It doesn't matter to me!! Windsor, Nova Scotia

I just wanted you to know about a corporate traveler of mine. I've had some weird request, but a few weeks ago this gentleman asked to be put on a night flight. . . Northside of the plane so he would "comet watch"!! I thought he was joking!! Woodbury, MN

A client came in and said, "I would like to sit by the *escape hatch*" I assumed he meant the exit row!! Hartford, CT

Upon returning a rental car the agent at the counter had an irate customer on the phone. This gentleman claimed to be locked inside the car and called numerous times for assistance from a cell phone. I asked the agent if anyone suggested that he roll down the window and open the door. When the agent made this suggestion, he hung up and didn't call again. I guess he got out of the car after all!! Chicago, IL

Would you believe a client called us from his flight to request a different seat assignment!! Norcross, GA

"Top 10 Questions Asked"

Another agent and I were flying from Minneapolis to Orlando on Northwest Airlines direct. She stopped the flight attendant and asked, "When would we by flying over Denver". Scary Huh!! Apple Valley, MN

I had a woman call and book a flight from Minneapolis to New York, John F Kennedy Airport. She then asked, "Will it take more than a day to get there"?!! Brooklyn Center, MN

I just had a phone call from a client that had purchased a round trip. She said, I won't be able to use the return portion of the ticket, will you buy it back from me"?!! Lexington, KY

"More Top Ten Questions"

10.   There was a Delta Flight departing Cincinnati at 9:30 PM to London. The client wanted to know what time dinner would be served and if she could eat before she got on the plane!! New Albany, TN

9.   A client asked, "How much it was to take the train from New Hampshire to Hawaii!! Dover, NH

8.   "Why can't you just tell the airlines that I purchased this ticket 21 days in advance even if I'm flying tomorrow"?!! Hartsville, SC

7.   When discussing the price in booking a mother and daughter to a resort in Jamaica, the mother informed me neither one of them was

married, so did that mean they had to pay the single supplement!! Warren, MI

6. From my client. . . "I would like to take a cruise form Orlando to Tampa, can you arrange that for me"?!! Orlando, FL

5. I got asked today, "If a British driver's license would be printed in English"?!! Tacoma, WA

4. My question was, "Can I get a Senior Citizen discount if I'm a Senior but not a citizen"?!! Ft Mill, SC

3. I had a man ask, "Can you call the airlines to tell them I'm dying so my daughter can get a lower fare. . . when he's perfectly healthy!! Allentown, PA

2.   A client planning her vacation in which a passport or certified birth certificate was required replies, "My birth certificate is 30 years old, is it still good"?!! Sterling, CO

1.   I made a reservation on a ticketless airline then faxed a copy to my client and highlighted the confirmation number "xyzlab". The secretary called back and asked, "When she checks in how does she pronounce those little marks"?!! Mayville, MO

"Top Ten Reasons to Answer an Ad for a Travel Agent Job"

10.   I have driven a truck before.!!

9.   I've sold windshields.!!

8.   I have a degree in Microbiology.!!

7.   I'm a part-time DJ in town.!!

6.   I can answer phones.!!

5.   I made hotel reservations while in the Army Reserve.!!

4.   I'm a waitress and worked at an Expresso Bar.!!

3.   I work at the Mt St Helens Visitor Center.!!

2.   I've worked a lot myself and the number one reason to answer an ad.!!

1.   I live with my sister who went through travel school.!!

Note: These are all true statements made by people who want to become travel agents!! Longview, WA

10.   A client called for information on Las Vegas. He asked, "What day of the week Thanksgiving was this year"? I said Thursday. He replied, "That can't be right, it was Thursday last year!! Knoxville, TN

9.   Is there any way to see Boston without actually going there!! Syracuse, NY

8. Are there sidewalks or do I have to walk in the road?!! Syracuse, NY

7. **When I go to New Brunswick, Canada, will I have a good time?!!** Syracuse, NY

6. **A client looking through a hotel brochure stated the rates day being 1-4 people. "Is the price stated meant for a quarter of a person"??!! Syracuse, NY**

5. **A client called to let me know that he left his jacket at the security point at Denver Airport and could you call and ask them to hold my jacket for me!!** St Paul, MN

4. **Requesting two one-way tickets, a client asked, "Can I pay for part of it now and pay the rest when I get back"??!!** Olathe, KS

3.   A client called to gather information about a trip and wanted "to go to an island that was surrounded by water"!! Ft Worth, TX

2.   A call from a gentleman asked, "Could I use the value of my ticket minus the $50.00 towards a bus ticket"??!! Bradford, PA

And the Number 1 Question of the Week:

1.   A man called wanting the earliest flight to Washington. I said there is one at 5:50AM. "Do you have one a little later"? I said yes, how about ten minutes to six....He said, "I'll take it"!! Albuquerque, NM

"Travel Terminology"

Today we had a client come in who had requested a "Gzeerer Rate". As he had talked to the agent more about his travel plans we realized he wanted none other than a Senior Coupon Book. Then right after that a woman called asking if we made plans to and from various places. Then she asked if she must pay us or could she just pay at the airport the day of departure. Must've been a full moon!! New Ulm, MN

I had a client call and ask for fares from Kansas City to San Diego. He wanted to go over Christmas, so in order to bring his fare down, I asked if he could stay over Saturday night. His response was, "At your house"!! Ft Leavenworth, KS

I book travel for a computer software company . . . People that you would think are fairly intelligent. . . Right? Well, I was telling a client that the plane from

Minneapolis to Rochford was a prop service. She asked what that meant and I said a propeller plane. She replied that she didn't know what that was! I said, "A very small plane that uses propellers to fly". She replied, OK but I still think she was confused!! Cincinnati, OH

When I worked at American as a reservation agent, I received a call from a little old lady advising me that we had forgotten her! I beg your pardon I replied. She repeated that we had forgotten her. She had been sitting outside her house all day waiting for the plane to pick her up! After seeing that she had a valid reservation, I booked her on a later flight. . . phoned a taxi to pick her up and told her that she would have to take the taxi to the airport for the plane!! Ruidoso, NM

A client called to request that a flight be waitlisted for her boss. Afterwards she said, "I am going to ask a stupid question". I replied that there was no such question. She asked, "Is that *weight* listed or wait listed"? I politely replied, "wait listed", and thought to myself "no such question until now"!! Norcross, GA

I had a customer ask me what an "airbus" meant on her itinerary. I explained it was a type of plane like a 747 or 737. She looked disappointed and said, "Oh, I thought a bus would come and pick me up at my house". It was hard to keep a straight face!! Costa Mesa, CA

I had a client call yesterday to inquire about an Amtrak trip he planned to and from Pensacola to Chicago. That route is on the cut list for September. He is going in July but also wants to go in November. He wants to buy his tickets for November now so he has them before they cut service. Go figure!! Warsaw, IN

"Would You Believe"

On the day of the O.J. Simpson verdict, October 3, 1995, a lady telephoned our Los Angeles reservation office and said, "I'm flying out today from St Louis to Los Angeles, I'll be in the air when the verdict is being read. She wanted to know if the pilot of the plane would let the passengers know the verdict. I told her that I did not know and that would be a decision made by the pilot. After a few moments of silence, she then asked me if I would contact the pilot and ask him or her to announce the verdict to the passengers, because she had missed a day of the trial. After a good laugh, I explained to her there was no way I could notify the pilot to make such an announcement. She was very upset and hung up!!
Los Angeles TWA Reservations

A client came in and wanted to purchase tickets to Madrid. He wanted to travel on 31 October. I told him if he traveled on 01 November, the fare was much lower. Since his flight departed at 7:00 PM, he wanted me to call the airline and see if they would honor the lower fare because it was on five hours from midnight!! Silver Springs, MD

I had a man come in clutching a picture of his cat. He asked me if I like cats and I replied, I had two of my own. He then burst into tears and cried for about ten minutes. When he regained his composure, he proceeded to tell me very graphically how his cat had been attacked by a coyote! He needed some very special travel arrangements and asked what I had considered peaceful destinations. I suggested several and he said he would think about them. The next day he said it was his cat's ashes and the reason for the trip was to sprinkle Tookie's ashes in a nice place. I didn't quite know what to say. I never had a dead cat on my desk before. He finally decided on Hollywood because his cat had loved going to the movies. I didn't want to ask about that one!! San Diego, CA

Last week a man shuffled into our office carrying a calculator. His clothing indicated he was probably a street person. He requested a cruise as he pulled a flyer from our brochure rack. "Something like this one" he said, indicating a $179.00 roundtrip air to Las Vegas. I gently informed him that what he held was not a cruise but a Las Vegas air package. Where upon he asked if the price included a hotel. At this point, I inquired as to what his actual travel needs were. He then held up the calculator and while pushing in several numbers, said his Board of Directors met last night and sent him to locate a hotel to be booked for a three-year stay. Did I think he could reserve one for say $51,000,000. I, of course, told him I thought it could be arranged and handed him his card to come back when he had a date and location. I would be happy to get him booked. Who could resist a $1.5 million commission!! Dallas, TX

A lady contacted our office to book a vehicle over the holiday weekend for a lengthy road trip. After checking some options, the lady called the next day advising the agent that her next door neighbor was kind enough to loan them their Suburban. However, they did not have a spare tire and she wanted to know if we could tell her where she could rent a spare tire for the weekend!! Duncan, OK

I had a client that wanted to take her pet with her on her trip. So after calling the airline, I quoted the rate of $65.00 per leg, not thinking that she would misunderstand. She then added up her dog's legs "4" and multiplied by $65.00 and came up with the Grand Total of $260.00. I almost lost it while she was calculating her costs!! Dallas, TX

This story is not going to be believed! A co-worker of mine got a phone call from a client stating that he had to transport a "Frozen Human Head" for a trial across the country and wanted to know what he had to do to clear it with the airlines so he would not be arrested. My co-worker laughed at him as he was a known client. She was sure he was joking! He wasn't! It seems that he works for counsel for a company that was sued by a man who somehow stapled his head with a staple gun and was now suing the maker of the gun. The lawyer was flying a head of a safety attachment and should have been safe if operated properly. I know it sounds crazy to you so you can imagine how the co-worker felt when she took the call!! Cincinnati, OH

One older gentleman wanted me to pre-assign him a seat. He was adamant about sitting next to a pretty blonde as he did not like brunettes!! Sparks, NV

Another client wanted me to make sure that the tray on the back of the seat in front of her worked properly as she didn't want her coffee to spill in her lap!! Sparks, NV

One last request was from a young Mother who wanted me to "Pre-Check" her in on her flights. Since she had her hands full with her kids, she couldn't possibly be bothered with the hassle of checking in her baggage and the kids at the same time. Go Figure!! Sparks, NV

I received a call from a gentleman inquiring about a trip to Las Vegas. I asked if he wanted air only or a package? He said he wanted a package. When I gave him the price for the package and the name of the hotel he asked, "Will the tour company allow my wife and I to stay at my sister-in-law's since we are going to visit them"?!! St Louis Park, MN

"Your Papers Please"

When I was a new agent, there was a rather impatient senior agent training me. She got upset when I would occasionally ask a client on the phone if I could work on his itinerary and call him back. At the time I found it necessary to do this if I was working on a complicated trip. One day the agent angrily asked me why I did this? I explained that sometimes I just needed time to think. Her quick response was, "In this business we don't have time to think"!! Framingham, MA

This one takes the cake! . . . A lady called to ask could she fax her daughter a copy of her birth certificate because the daughter was flying to Canada in a few days. I advised that she needed a certified copy of the birth certificate or even an old passport. The Mother told me her daughter never bought a passport because they cost too much. I then suggested over-nighting the certificate. The Mother then explains her daughter is a flight attendant and she didn't have a place she could send the Fed Ex. We couldn't already have a passport or know the requirements for traveling outside the U.S!! Chattanooga, TN

"Wouldn't You Love to Say"

A fax came across my desk this morning with travel industry. . . Comments you would love to say to clients but can't:

1. No, I'm telling you this because I'm bored.!!
2. When the airlines are good and ready.!!
3. Well, this is 1996, not when bread was a nickel!!
4. Cuz they don't, that's why.!!
5. Cuz that's what it cost.!!
6. Yes ma'am/sir. I do care about your personal life story but for now which flight do you want.!!
7. Yes, I can discount this, however, will you make our payroll this week.!!

8. Here he/she comes again. . . where's the booking?!!

9. Questions. . Questions. . where's the booking?!!

10. Yes, it was cheaper last week. Why didn't you buy then?!!

11. Tuff!!!

Our travel agency, aside from booking unusual flights, Amtrak and tours, also organizes private fully escorted bus trips. On a recent trip to Niagara Falls, I was reconfirming pick up times and locations for everyone on the bus. I also reminded everyone to bring their birth certificate or voters registration due to the fact that we were crossing the border into Canada. One lady mistakenly thought I said to bring "Birth Control". I laughed and said that you never know just what border patrol may want to see!! Mifflintown, PA

Today I had someone call requesting an upgrade to first class. She said he would be using a certificate. I inquired what type of upgrade certificate and her response, "It's white with brown ink on it"!! Cambridge, MA

I was booking a gentleman to Los Angeles. After completing his reservation, he asked if his passport had to be valid. I said, "Why would that matter"? and he replied, "I thought you needed a passport for Los Angeles since they are all the way on the other side of the country and there is so much international activity over there. This guy worked for CNN!! Cary, NC

While working on my first job as a travel agent I was proud that I worked in the oldest travel agency in existence that prides itself on being full-service. I received a call from a gentleman that had read our ad in the yellow pages and as a result forcefully requested that I secure a "fishing license" so that he could bass fish on his vacation that was to take place 50 miles from home on a lake that is about one mile from the licensing office!! Birmingham, AL

"Travel Doo-Opp Song"

A little travel agent Ditty called "Travel Agents Life"
to be sung to the tune of "Mack the Knife":

"When the phone rings

half past eight dear

you may moan and roll your eyes

just another inquiring traveler

wanting frequent flyer flights

printing tickets

Don't mean nothing

with luck dear fare will dive

and you'll be printing one more ticket.

You can probably bet your life

Booking Hotels

Round the World now

But the lady wants a suite

Don't you dare dear charge more money

Cause you hear it should be free

then the phone rings.

It's your Mother

wants to fly home for Christmas eve

since you're the agent of the family

it should be commmmmmmmmplimentarareeeee

XXX all together now for the finale XXX

when the clock strikes

half past five dear

you can sign off and breathe a sigh

it's been another average day here

in the travel agent's life….yea.!!

Columbus, GA

LaVergne, TN USA
30 August 2010
195045LV00001B/10/A